Apart from Our Our

Own
The Machines

A. R. Fisher

Chapter 1

It was a muggy, humid summer day. After school, my friend Penny calls me up asking me if I wanted to meet up with her, Mickey and Petey at the elementary school. I said sure.

After dinner I headed out and took a flashlight for comfort. I cut through the path behind our neighbors yard. The tall grass brushed against my legs and made them itchy. I got to the sidewalk and saw Mickey and Penny on the swings. When I reached the swings I saw Petey coming over.

Penny and I were sitting on the swings while Petey and Mickey were leaning against the poles of the swing set. The four of us started talking about the memories on the playground even though they have updated since we were here. As it got darker the light poles that surrounded the playground started turning on.

"Okay now that's cool."

We all looked at each other, then Mickey.

"What?" he said.

We started to laugh. "Let's play a game."

"Like what?"

"I don't know, hide a seek. There's bound to be a lot of places to hide."

"Sure, one, two, three, not it."

"Not it," the rest of us said.

"Penny you said it last, go count."

She started counting and the rest of us hid. I found an obvious spot. It was so obvious I knew she wouldn't find me.

She found Mickey first, then Petey. I could see all three of them looking in all the wrong spots. "Moni, you better be on the wood chips."

"I am on the woodchips," I yelled.

"Dude, where are you?"

"On the woodchips."

"Duh, I give up."

"Oh you're no fun," I said getting up. I was on the jungle gym, and my hiding spot was lying on the floor of the play set. I looked down at her.

"That will be the first spot I look next time."

Chapter 2

The four of us were hanging out on the swings. The woods were behind us, and so was the fence that separated us from the woods. A warm, refreshing breeze blew and rattled the fence. The four of us became silent, and we looked to where the sound came from.

"I think it's time for us to leave," Mickey suggested.

"I think you're right," I said terrified, still looking to where the sound came from.

A loud crack of a tree branch shot me off the swing. Penny held my hand and we squeezed the life out of each other's hand. The four of us backed up to a slide and got behind it. The breeze had stopped and the air became humid and stale. Each breath of air hurt my chest and throat. Penny looked to me and put her arm around my shoulders. "Moni, are you okay?"

"No," I said holding my chest. "It just got really cold, it's hard to breath."

I laid my head on her shoulder, and she laid me down. I was staring at the bottom of the slide. "Moni."

I closed my eyes and was walking through tall metal buildings. I was standing on a balcony and saw they weren't buildings. They were machines. I was in a world apart from our own. I was staring at this strange world from the balcony. I saw one machine tower over the others. As I starred closer I saw a black hand grab me. It pulled me to the tower, and then stopped. I opened my eyes and saw Penny.

I woke up screaming, and hit my head on the slide when I sat up. I felt hands grab my arms and legs.

"Moni, it's okay."

I slowly came back to reality. My breathing was still heavy and my head was pounding. I turned to Penny, and the hands let go of me. I looked away. I franticly found her hand and held it tight.

"Let's get her off the woods chips."

I closed my eyes as they were moving me and somehow I fell asleep.

Penny

I was holding Moni, looking at Petey and Mickey. We we're all clueless to what was wrong. We all hope that she is okay.

Chapter 3

Moni

I was looking at Penny. She was strapped to the center of this circle. She wasn't moving and her head hung low. She was pale and was fading fast. She couldn't lift her head to see me, even though I think she knew I was there. I heard the machine turn on and Penny come to "life." Her body stiffened, her face lifted to the sky, Her eyes were wide open and her mouth was trying to scream, but no sound came out. The circle behind her turned orange, and her eyes glowed. I was being pushed away by the same hand that wanted to me to see it.

I opened my eyes to see the playground. Through my half open eyes I looked at the swing set, and the jungle gym. I was holding Penny's hand and the boys weren't there. I sat up.

"You okay?"

I turned to Penny, "what happened?"

"I think I should be asking you that question."

"It was a nightmare," I said sitting up.

"But, you weren't asleep?"

"I sure felt asleep?"

"Your eyes were wide open," she told me.

"I saw another world. It was different then ours, and they took you."

"Moni, it was only a dream."

"I was in it too."

"Of course you were. It was your dream."

"It's going to happen."

"You don't really believe that, do you?" she questioned.

"I do." I stood up and slowly went over to the swings. The boys came back and stood in front of me.

"Everything okay?" Petey asked.

"Yeah," I said looking at the ground.

"That was convincing," Mickey said.

"Go ask Penny. I already told her."

I watched them walk over to her and the three of them start to talk. I was sitting on the swings with my back to the woods, when I heard a very quiet click in the distance. I looked over my shoulder and out the corner of my eye. I stood up and went over to the fence. I looked into the dark trees. I took a few steps back and saw a small white dot just floating in mid-air. I sat back on the swing and starred at the dot. It grew slightly with every passing second. After five minutes or so it quickly grew to twice its size. It lit up the playground, and got the attention of Penny, Petey, and Mickey. I stood up and Penny helped me as we walked backwards until we were against the slides. The light got brighter and I walked towards it. I stood only a few feet away from the light. While the white light was hypnotizing me, I was blind to the black dot that was forming in the middle of the white circle. The dot was slowly coming closer and was forming into a hand. I eventually saw the hand but I couldn't move. I wasn't in control of my body. The hand was reaching for me but I couldn't do anything about it.

Chapter 4

The hand was coming closer and I still hadn't moved. I felt a shove from my left, and then everything was silent.

I picked myself up from the woods chips and looked to Mickey and Petey.

"Are you okay?" Petey asked coming over.

"Where's Penny?"

They were silent. I went over to a slide and carelessly sat down. They came over and Petey knelt down. "What did you see?"

"Nothing, when?"

"Before, behind the slide," he pointed.

"That hand, and Penny being taken."

"Is that it?" he asked patiently.

"No. We, she and I, were in a different world. That world," I pointed to where the portal appeared.

"Well then, I guess we are going to have to get you in there."

"How?"

"I know a guy," he said taking his phone out. He walked to the other side of the playground.

"Did you know about any of this?" I asked looking at Mickey.

"Of what? I do a lot of research, but this is way out of my field of interest."

"To think that we played on this playground when we went to school here"

"I heard my mom saying something about children disappearing. Do you think this is what has been happening?"

"Could be," Mickey said.

"Who did you call?" I asked Petey as he came back over.

"My brother. He said this is probably what has been happening to the kids. He also said that going into this world is suicide."

"I don't have a choice. Penny is in there because I was to stubborn to move."

"It wasn't your fault. Danny did say that there is a way to force the portal open."

"Let's do it," I said.

"I'm coming with you," Petey said.

I slightly smiled. "Where is this thing to open the portal?"

"On a tree's trunk."

"So like over the fence?" I asked.

"Like over the fence," he repeated.

The three of us went to the fence and started to climb over. There was barbwire at the top. We stopped at the top. "Now what."

"I'm not going to let her die."

I climbed through the stiff wire. It ripped my clothes and drew blood from my veins. We got to the other side and Petey looked at my arms.

"I'm fine, let's find this thing."

My arms gently slide out of Petey's grip, leaving my blood on his palms as I walked away. We split it up and found it with no time to spare. I turned to Petey and he pointed to Mickey. We both walked to Mickey's tree. I looked at the metal panel on the tree trunk.

"No one has spotted this?"

"Apparently not."

"What now?"

"We open the portal," Petey said.

"Easier said than done," Mickey said.

"What are you talking about?"

"Take a look."

Petey stood behind us and all good emotions left his face. "How do we figure this out?"

"I can help with that," we heard from behind us.

Chapter 5

"Danny, you came," Petey said.

"Anything for my brother."

"Oh, Moni this is Danny, my older brother. He's going to help us get the portal back open."

I smiled and looked to the tree. Danny got closer to get a better look. "Okay, I figured it out, but I can't do anything until the person who is going into the world is in the spot where Penny was when she was taken. Who's going?"

"I am," I raised my hand.

"I'm coming," Petey said.

"You don't have to."

"I want to."

We got ourselves back over the fence and stood in the spot where Penny was taken. "Are you guys ready?"

"We don't have a choice. Yes we are ready," I said. I held Petey's hand as the portal started to appear.

"Be careful," Danny said. "Don't touch the machines, and you have to be out before sunrise before the portal closes for good, and you become trapped like the others."

"Others?"

The hand came toward us and I wasn't going to be pushed by Penny. My grip on Petey's hand tightened as the hand came closer. It grabbed me, but Petey held on. It quickly pulled us into the portal. I looked behind me, and the playground was gone. I looked to Petey, "Are we doing the right thing?"

My voice came out echoed. I pulled Petey closer to the hand and he grabbed on. *How much longer?* I turned to the way the hand was coming from. *Seems endless.*

I woke up on a cold, hard ground. I was looking at the amber colored sky, in the breaks of giant shadows. I sat up slowly, and held my head. "The machines."

When my eyes were in focus I saw Petey on his side. I slowly crawled over and sat behind him, then laid him on my lap. While holding him, I looked around.

"Are, guys, kay?"

"Mickey?"

"Yeah, me."

"You keep breaking up," I said.

"Kay, hold."

The world was quiet and suspenseful. It felt like I was in a horror movie, but this was for real.

"Can you hear me now?"

"Much better."

"Are you guys okay?"

"I am."

"Petey?"

"He's not waking up?" I looked down at him and held his hand.

"Where are you?"

"I don't know."

I heard a beep. "I was able to get a map. I can see you and Petey."

"What am I suppose to do?"

"Nothing, let's take this one step at a time. Wake Petey up and we will go from there."

I heard a click, like someone hanging up a phone.

"Petey," I said looking down at him. I could see pain in his relaxed body. "Petey, please wake up." I saw a tear stream to his hair and his body slowly took motion. "Are you okay?"

"Yeah, my head hurts. What happened?"

"I don't know. When I woke up we were here."

"Where is here?" he asked.

I helped him up and put his arm around my shoulder. "Mickey."

I got nothing.

"Mickey," I said a little louder.

"He's back home Moni."

"No, he and I were talking before."

"Moni, I'm right here. Is Petey awake?"

"Yeah man, right here," Petey said.

I smiled a little. "Where do we go?"

"You have to find a shelter. That's the half way mark. You guys have to understand the challenges you will encounter, before and after the shelter."

"We both understand the challenges and consequences, but we don't have a choice."

The speaker clicked and we started off finding a path through the unforgiving machines. We walked at his pace towards a few tall buildings. There were two on the right, and two on our left. There was an alleyway on both sides. We looked down one alleyway, then the other.

"Take the right one," Mickey radioed in.

Petey and I looked at each other before going down the dark, damp alleyway. He gave me a slight smile, and then we started off. While we walked between the buildings I felt very short of breath. I have never been claustrophobic. My breathing turned to hyperventilating.

"Moni," I heard Petey say.

"No water?" I asked between breaths.

"No water," he repeated.

I sat down and was starting to lie down. Petey stopped me and sat with his legs under my head. "The shelter will have water. I promise."

"And if it doesn't?" I asked.

"Then we will have to rough it," he said. "How you feeling?"

"Better, we have to go."

He helped me up then picked me up. "I'm okay."

"I know," he said.

Chapter 6

We got to the end of the alley and stood on a sidewalk that led in both directions. "Mickey."

"Left and when you get to the balcony that over looks the machines go all the way down the walkway and the last door on your left is the one you want. There should be stairs behind the door."

Petey and I walked hand-in-hand to the balcony. The view was so unbelievable. We stood at the railing and overlooked thousands of machines. There was one machine that towered over the others. "Is that the one your brother told us about?"

"I guess it is."

I starred at the machine and saw the Black Hand reach for me. It pulled me to face Penny. She looked into my eyes. I looked to a robot arm that was to her right. They were doing something with her arm and a needle. I looked back to her eyes. I could feel a pinch on my arm as we yelled to the sky. I heard thunder and saw a streak of lightning.

"Moni, wake up."

I was on Petey's lap, his arms around me. "We have to hurry."

"What did you see?"

"It was weird. I think a stronger bond has formed between her and I."

"What does that mean?"

"I can see her, when she's not really here. I can feel any pain she goes through, and she will lead the way for us to find her."

We both got up and went to our next location. The stairs. We followed the balcony all the way to the end, and opened the door. We went downstairs, and Mickey was giving us the next set of directions.

"The next door you will open will be the start of the machine journey," Mickey said slow and low.

Petey put his hand on the knob and looked to me. I looked in his eyes, then down to the floor. He held my hand and lifted my chin. He wiped away the tears and hugged me close.

"It's okay to be scared," he said.

"I can't be scared. I need to be brave for Penny."

"Are you forgetting that you have someone you can lean on, to turn to through all of this?"

"I guess I am," I said laying my head on his shoulder. One of his hands was on my back, the other on my neck. After I let everything out, we went over to the door again. "Just do it."

He turned the handle and pulled it open. The world was quiet as we took a few steps out. I looked back to the door.

"No looking back. It was you that said we didn't have a choice," he said. We passed the first pair of machines there were on either side of us, "And so it begins."

Chapter 7

A few hours had gone by and we stopped to rest. I was kneeling down with him on my lap. "We only have until morning. We can't stop for long."

"Let's go," he said getting up. He held his hand out to me. I smiled up at him. We walked for a short while, and the brick shelter came into view. It looked to be a mile at the longest. Petey and I stood in that spot for a little bit, just taking it in.

"Almost," I encouraged.

I put his arm around my shoulders and we pressed forward.

The machines hissed, and it felt like they were watching us. I looked up at them, which I knew I shouldn't have done. I stopped and took his arm off my shoulders.

"Moni, what's wrong?"

While I was looking up, into what appeared to be eyes, I could hear them, and hear Penny. I could see her strapped to the center of the circle. I saw the needle in her arm that was attached to a small plastic tube. The tube was filled with her blood. I tried to touch her hair, her face, but I knew I wasn't real.

When I woke up we were in front of the brick shelter. I was hoping it would be bigger. He looked down at me and put my feet on the ground. He opened the door and we slowly walked in. It was very messy and old. The brick outside was in better shape than the inside walls. He sat against the wall while I looked around. I stepped over metal beams and plastic tubes. There were screws and bolts scattered under the clutter. Within the clutter I saw a refrigerator lying on its side. I climbed over metal scarps and fell onto the fridge. I got up and pulled open the door. It was empty.

"Did you find something?" Petey asked.

"I thought I found water."

"Did you?"

"No," I said pulling open the other draw. "Wait, hold on. I found two bottles. One for us and one for Penny."

"Throw one over here."

"Did you hear what I said?"

"Yeah, I won't drink the whole thing. My stomach can't handle that right now."

We were both against the wall. I was starring at the opposite wall. I took a small drink, and then asked Petey what time it was. I didn't get an answer. I looked to him and his eyes were closed. "Petey, are you okay?"

I touched his shoulder and gently laid him on my lap. I knew he was dehydrated, but we don't have enough to get us back home. I tried to get water in him, but he wouldn't wake up.

"Is everything okay?" Mickey buzzed in.

"No, we found water, but not enough for us and Penny. Petey is passed out because of dehydration, and I'm close to passing out too. Danny, tell me what to do."

Chapter 8

We were still in the shelter and poor Petey was still unconscious. I picked his wrist up and saw it was two in the morning. I looked to his face and saw a thin layer of dirt under a layer of sweat and maybe a few tears.

I was in a moment of looking at Petey when I heard a thud on the door. "Who's there?"

I looked up at the ceiling and prayed to Danny. The thud came again, but louder. I didn't know what to do. I was frozen in fear. I lifted Petey's torso, and cradled his head while I held him close. I bent my knees up to support his back. I looked to my right and there was a large cloth with a few holes in it. The blanket was better cover than nothing at all. I put it over us as I heard a third thud. The door flew open and a robotic hand came in. That hand reminded me of the Black Hand in my visions. *Could that be the hand?* As abruptly as the hand came, it left, leaving the door wide open. I uncovered us and looked down at Petey. Still nothing. As I got up I rolled up the blanket and put it under Petey's head. I slowly went over and very quietly shut the door. When I got back to where I was sitting I picked the water up. I sat next to Petey and carefully sat him up. I took the lid off and put the top of the water bottle to his lips. The water was able to quench his thirst. He coughed as he sat up, and sprayed water. I gave him that water and told him to finish it.

"Moni, are you sure? What about you?"

"I'm fine I just want to get to Penny. Are you okay to walk?"

"Give me a few minutes. I just woke up."

"Was it dehydration?"

"Yeah, that and exhaustion," he said taking another sip.

I waited by the door and watched him drink the final sips of the water. *There's no going back now*, I thought to myself. I caught myself smiling when I saw him get up. I went over and helped him. I took the empty bottle from his hand and put it on the ground. Just in case I folded the blanket the best I could and put it over one shoulder. Petey stumbled to the door and I followed close behind.

"I have an extra shoulder. You should take it slow."

He turned back to me with one hand on the wall. He was slouched over, but was looking at me. He sounded so out of breath.

"Are you sure you're okay to go on?"

"No, but do I have a choice?"

I looked to the ground and turned to the door. I looked at the knob and slowly turned it. I cracked the door and looked around. I held my hand out to him. I pulled him lightly so I could put his around my shoulder. We slowly opened the door and started towards Penny.

When we took our five-minute break I sat him down. I looked at the path ahead and could see the machine that had Penny. I turned around and Petey was leaning against something. I looked at Petey, and then looked up. The machine stopped working and I heard a drum like sound. I went to Petey and picked him up. The drum sound went away. I looked up at the machine and it had gone back to work.

"What was that?" the speaker came on.

"It was the machine."

"Couldn't have been," Danny said. "Machine don't have heartbeats."

"Oh, I thought it was a drum?"

"He touched the machine, so now his heartbeat is recorded and stored," he explained.

"What does that mean for him?"

"Nothing yet. The closer you get to Penny, the more in danger Petey will be."

"There is no cutting us a break. Is there?" I said submissively and pulled back my greasy hair. I gently let go of Petey's arm and he bent over to support his own weight.

"The best thing right now is to relax. Let's focus on one thing at a time. Let's get to Penny and go from there."

"Okay," I said grabbing Petey's arm again.

"I'm okay," Petey said.

"You sure."

"I don't want you to carry me," he said.

I smiled and we pressed forward. We walked closer and closer to the death trap that was waiting for us on the other side.

Chapter 9

Petey was starting to feel heavy on my shoulders. I looked forward and could see Penny. "Come on Petey, we are almost there."

We pushed on until we were standing at the base of the machine that had Penny. I put Petey on the ground away from the machines and looked around. The story of the disappearances has been solved. I went over to the enclosed prison and a blonde haired girl slid her hand through the bars. She was dirt covered, had torn clothes and had tear filled eyes.

"I'm Moni," I said softly.

"Jeana," she said shyly.

"Is everyone okay?"

"All but one," she said and turned to a boy lying on the ground shivering. I gave her the blanket we took from the shelter. She gave it to the boy and sat down next to him. I glanced over each face that was behind bars, and then looked up to Penny. The white background on the machine turned orange. She was looking at the sky and I felt a pinch on my inner arm. I looked down and a small line of blood ran down my arm to my wrist.

"How do we get her down?"

"That's a good question," Jeana said. "None of us have ever seen anything like this."

"Petey, we have to get her down."

"Moni, I, I can't come with you. I can't touch them again."

"I'll go. You have to get them out," I said pointing to the prison door.

"The keys are up there." Jeana said looking up to Penny.

"I'll drop them when I get up there."

I brought Petey over to the metal bars and sat him down. I walked backwards a little bit, and then turned to face the machine. I looked to see a ladder, or stairs, but there were none. I took a deep breath, and started up.

About half way up there was a platform I rested on for a few seconds. I sat down and opened the water bottle. While I was leaning against the machine I could very faintly hear my heartbeat in the background. I got up and faced the machine. I looked up and saw Penny. I turned to see the path I wanted to take. I looked behind me and saw the other machines. I took a deep breath and started climbing. I felt weaker now then when I was on the platform. I could hear my heartbeat echo through the machines. It was like one machine records it, and all the other machines get it too.

I forced myself to reach the top. I was pass Penny and was so close to the top. I stood on its flat surface and looked down. I didn't look down after that. I lifted my head and saw the keys at the end of the ledge that was jutting out from the machine. The width of the ledge was the size of a balance bean. I looked at the keys and started out.

"Moni, what are you doing?" Petey yelled.

I focused on the keys. I was in an arms distance, but got closer to be sure. I stopped and started to reach when they moved away. Without thinking I jumped onto the arm that held the keys. I wrapped my legs around it and pulled myself up. While it was moving, I carefully scooted myself to the hand. The keys dangled, waiting to be dropped. When I got to the hand I knew I had to open the fingers to get the keys out. Once I got the key ring free I let the keys drop to the ground, then started to make my way back to the machine's flat roof.

I was standing on the top of the machine and looked at Penny. I was trying to figure out how to get down to her. I saw another arm come out and move towards her arm. The arm was wide and thick. I backed up from the edge a few steps and readied myself. I took those steps forward and jumped off, and was now falling towards the arm. When I landed on it I hugged it to make sure I wasn't going anywhere. I sat on the arm and looked at my inner elbows and the sides of my knees. I hugged the arm so tight I have cuts that are slowly leaking blood. I looked up and I was getting closer to her. I moved myself to the end. The arm stopped when it got to her arm. I looked at the locks on her hands. They didn't have a keyhole, but the locks on her ankles did. There was nothing for me to hold onto to get off the arm to help her. I looked down and saw that the kids were no longer behind bars.

"I need the keys," I yelled.

I saw Petey give the keys to Jeana. She ran to the base of the machine, and out of sight. When I heard a thumping sound in the distance I knew she was climbing up.

The arm was attaching another vile to the needle. When it was done it started to move away.

"No," I held my hand up to Penny. I was looking around trying to find something to grab onto. Without knowing where to jump, I jumped. I was able to grab the bar that attached her ankle locks together. I knew one day my upper body strength would be the death of me. My hands were sweaty and losing grip. I looked up to Penny and asked her for help. I looked down at the group and saw Petey unconscious.

"I can't do this," I said looking back up to Penny. I teared up, closed my eyes and let go.

Chapter 10

With my eyes closed I saw flashbacks of everything in my thirteen years of life, then everything went black. I opened my eyes, and wrapped around my body was the Black Hand from my visions. It was bringing me back to her.

I was at her height and was close enough to take the needle out of her arm. I took the vile off and detached the tube. I felt drained and so weak. The white background behind Penny turned orange, and the amber sky disappeared behind gray smoke. I moved my tired eyes back down to Penny. She was looking up to the sky. Her eyes and mouth were open and glowing, then she didn't move. I still felt weak but at the same time I could feel certain energy within me.

Jeana

I was holding Petey, looking up at Moni and her friend.

"Moni, what is that?"

"This is Jeana," I told the radio voice coming from nowhere.

"Where is Moni, and Petey?" the voice asked worried.

"Petey is unconscious, and something truly amazing is happening to Moni."

The clouds let out rain while Moni and her friend's energy reflected into the sky. The other kids ran for cover while I stood up with Petey in my arms. I starred in amazement as I saw Moni's spirit break way from her body. Her body slowly floated to the ground while her spirit started to unlock her friend. Over the pitter-patter of rain, I heard each lock click open. Moni touched her friend's chest and an orange spirit broke free from her friend's body, and then her body floated to the ground.

I looked up to their spirits with the Black Hand under Moni's feet. It slowly came down and rested on the ground. Moni looked at me and she was holding her friend the same exact way I was holding Petey. Moni was next to her friend's body, and gently laid her in her body. She stood at her body's feet, still standing on the Black Hand. She looked at me and pointed to her body. I gently put Petey on the ground and pulled her body closer to the Black Hand, and then she pointed back to Petey.

"It's four-thirty. The portal is open for two more hours. You guys need to hurry." The phone clicked and the rain started to slow down. I was under an overhang with Petey in my arms and my hand on his chest. His heart, beat with mine. I looked out to Moni and her friend. I saw motion in her friend's body and the Black Hand slowly disappeared from where I laid. Petey and I went out to her. She opened her eyes and starred up. The rain stopped, but the clouds remained. I put my one hand on her shoulder. "Are you okay?"

She looked at me in a daze, and then she saw Petey. She slowly sat up with the help of my hand. When she was up she gave me a confused look. "I'm Jeana."

"Weren't you the first one taken?"

"Yes, I don't want to talk about it. I feel so blessed right now. How did you guys get here?"

"Don't ask me. Moni is the true hero.

I helped her up as much as I could without dropping Petey, and the three of us went to Moni. Penny sat on one side and I sat on the other. I held Petey's head and let his body relax on the ground. The other kids came out from their cover, and we waited.

Chapter 11

Moni

I woke up on the hard ground with Penny on one side, and Jeana on the other. The kids that Petey had freed surrounded us. Penny sat me up and I looked down at Petey. I took him from Jeana's arms and slowly stood up. I looked up to the machine that held Penny. The white light turned off and the ground shook hard.

"You guys need to get out now. The portal is starting to close," I heard over the rumbles and crashes. I rallied everyone together to follow me.

"Penny, the closest escape portal is two miles from here."

"Well, I guess we better get going then."

I was able to smile. I missed her sense of courage in trying times. The ground shook at times, and when it did it was impossible to do anything or move anywhere except with the shakes of the ground. During the earthquakes we stopped and I looked down at Petey. His eyes were slightly open. I smiled and put my hand on his cheek. His eyes grew wider as he grabbed my shirt and rolled away from that machine. We looked at each other, and then at the huge piece of metal that was now in our place.

"Now we are even," he said. "Let's go."

I got off him and helped him up. Penny took my hand and pulled me behind her.

"Petey, come on," I yelled. As Penny was pulling me away, Petey dropped to his knees. I ripped my hand out of Penny's grip and ran back to him. "Petey, you have to get up, Come on."

"No, I can't," he said. "My life has been in jeopardy the whole adventure. It's time for you to go," he told me. Penny's hand grabbed mine as I slowly walked backwards.

I was running behind Penny when I re-saw what I just did. "I can't do this."

I turned back alone and sprinted back to Petey. He was lying on the ground. I saw an overhang right beside us and brought him over. I put him on my lap and cradled his head. I brought him closer to me and laid my cheek on the top of his head. I pulled his legs closer to me and watched the world crumble around us. I could feel tears coming and the fear take over. I hugged him tight. "We aren't going to make it Petey."

He lay so still. He didn't know what was going on. He couldn't hear me praying. The ground shook continuously and I pushed myself into the corner. I held him so tight and closed my eyes while rocking back and forth. The huge metal pieces have blocked our way out. I looked to the gray clouds and amber sky and saw a black hand. I relaxed all emotion and focused on the hand. It slowly came down, lay on the ground and waited. I sniffled, wiped a few tears, and got up with Petey in my arms. I walked over to the hand and hesitated to step on. I looked at Petey then down to the hand and stepped up. I put Petey down, and when the hand started moving up I sat down because I didn't have very good balance. I held his hand and smiled knowing we are alive and we are going to make it out. I looked to where the hand was coming from. It was from the balcony, and between the buildings. I looked back and the machines had started to topple over. The sight was unbelievable. I looked forward and we were retracing our steps from before. We passed the black alleyway, and between the buildings, then the ground where we woke up in this place. It was all behind us now. We were in the portal again. Petey was fuzzy and the colors of the portal passed by quickly. I laid down, still holding Petey's hand and closed my eyes. I saw us at the playground. Penny and the others were waiting at the entrance of the portal. I saw me on the ground and everyone surround me.

"Moni," I heard faintly. I slowly opened my eyes and saw a light, dark blue sky, and Penny.

"Where am I?"

"You're home," Petey said.

I suddenly became very awake and sat up quickly. "Petey, you're okay?"

"Yeah, and it's all thanks to you."

"Moni, take it easy."

"Did we get everyone out?"

I looked around and saw the little boy in front holding the blanket. He walked towards me and put the blanket on my legs. He knelt down next to me and quickly gave me a hug. I wrapped my arms around him.

"Because of you, I can finally see my mommy again," he said.

Tears came to my eyes as Petey helped me up. Mickey and Danny came forward. Danny went to Penny and touched her shoulders. "You don't need to use your strength right now."

Mickey picked her up and I felt a tap on my shoulder. It was Jeana. "I don't know how to thank you. It has taken my years to figure out how to get out, and you did it in one night. You're a hero."

Danny and Petey took my arms off their shoulders and I hugged the girl who had to grow up before she needed to. I looked her in the eyes and we turned to go home.

"Come home with us and we will get everyone to the hospital."

The five of us stood on the porch as I rang the doorbell. My brother answered the door. "I'll tell you later. We all should get to the hospital. I'll say that we have solved the mystery of the disappearing children. I'll tell you about the adventure later."

Chapter 12

I woke up in a hospital room with Ryan, my brother, by my side. I slowly sat up and saw Penny in the bed next to me.

"What happened?" I asked Ryan.

"I am finding this out just like you are. I gave them permission to take blood. You and Penny have the same blood type," he said.

I looked to Penny. "Where is everyone?"

"In their rooms. If you feel up to it, we can go see Petey," Ryan said.

I flung the covers off and put my feet on the ground. "Let's go."

I looked at Penny as we passed by.

We got to Petey's room and Danny was there with Mickey.

"How's he doing?" I asked.

"He'll have to stay one more night, but he's stable right now," Danny said.

"Parents coming?"

"They can't. They were killed in a car crash last summer."

"Petey never said anything?"

"He never does."

Danny looked down to him, and so did I. I put my hand on his hand, then moved it to feel his heartbeat. *Maybe we were meant to be more than friends.* I enclosed my hand around his, and took a step closer toward his head. I leaned over the railing on the side of the bed and kissed his forehead, then his lips. I felt him kiss me back. We ended the kiss and I looked in his eyes.

"Thank you," he said.

I smiled, kissed him on the head and told him to rest. I turned towards the door and saw Jeana holding hands with the little boy. "Is he your brother?"

"I know I didn't seem like a sister to him in the other world. I was just so scared that I might have lost him. Yes he is my brother. Thank you again. How is Petey doing?"

"They are going to keep him one more night to be sure," I said looking back to Petey.

"I would like you to meet someone," she said.

She brought me out into the lobby and there were two adults. "These are my parents. They wanted to meet the person who brought me home."

"We can't thank you enough, or understand that fact of risking your life to save her and the other kids." *I went in for a different reason and picked them up on the way.*

I heard footsteps behind me. My group of friends was standing behind me now. Jeana had begun to walk the other way. I turned to look to my friends and Penny came up to me. "You saved my life."

"I didn't have a choice. It was either you or me, and I chose me. I wasn't going to lose you." I wiped a tear away before it fell. She put her hand on my shoulder and brought me in for a well needed hug. She hugged me so tight and I gave the same pressure back to her. After the hug she kept her arm around my shoulders and we walked back to Petey's room. He was awake in his bed, and was sitting up talking to Danny. I felt a presence at the door. I turned around.

"Which one of you is Moni?"

"I am," I said raising my hand.

"You have been requested back to the lobby," the nurse said.

"Hold on, I want to come with you," Petey said.

"Uh, I don't think the doctors want you out of bed," I said.

"Does it look like I care what the doctors want me to do right now. I'm coming," he said starting to get up.

We walked to the lobby and there were parents sitting in chairs and the children I rescued were coming out into the lobby. I stood by the door, feeling a little out of place, but filled with happiness and something else. I can't really describe it.

"Is that her?"

"That's her," a little girl said.

The parents came up to me with arms open, and hands held out. I was getting individual thank yous from the mothers and fathers, brothers and sisters. As the last pair of parents was walking down the hall I remembered that this adventure would have not been a success if it weren't for the people standing next to me. Penny was on my right with her mom behind her. Mickey was on the other side of her with his mom and brother. Petey was to my left with his brother, and of course Danny was behind me. He put his hand on my shoulder and I looked up at him as I put my hand on his hand.

"I think we are good on adventures for a while."

"Yeah, not really," Petey said.

"Ha, yeah, as soon as this one is over, we'll find some other world to destroy," Penny chuckled.

When she said that it got me wondering. *Are there other worlds within our world, and are they ready yet to be discovered?*

The adventures continue in

Apart from Our

Own
Reflections

www.ingramcontent.com/pod-product-compliance
Lightning Source LLC
Chambersburg PA
CBHW050915120626
46552CB00004B/1585